Morningstar Musings

DANICA GIM

MORNINGSTAR MUSINGS
Copyright © 2018 by Danique Gimbrère. All rights reserved. This book or any portion thereof may not be reproduced or used in any manner whatsoever without the express written permission of the writer except for the use of brief quotations in a book review.

Cover art (inspired on a picture by Andres Melo) and chapter illustrations by Margaret le Jarde.

Illustrations by Gabrielle Moran.

Author picture by Andres Melo.

Revisions by Arlette Krijgsman.

ISBN-13: 978-1979734998

@danica.gim

/danicagim

www.danicagim.com

*For **you.***

*In your raven hair I found sunshine
in the black of your eyes I found stars
in every darkness of your features
I found an ocean full of light.*

Introduction

The words within these pages have been written far away from home. It's about the struggle of a journey, of a life in two worlds. This is about discovering a new reality with new realizations. About an old love I thought would last forever and a new love that relighted a fire in my soul I thought to be gone for good. This is about my femininity and how society treats it. About my vulnerability as I question my religion and with that everything I was taught.

This book is for everyone who ever travelled and who found themselves between two homes. For the ones that discovered new love and had to learn to let go of the old. This is for the writers, the poets, the painters, the dreamers. For the ones with lovers on a distance and a battlefield in their hearts.

This is for all of you who have been brave enough to start over while going against everything you have ever known.

Thank you for reading this piece of me. I'll be holding your hand through the pages.

Love,

Danica / Danique

P.s. I left these blank pages for you. Write and draw your heart out. This book belongs to you now, as much as its words once belonged to me.

DA • NI • CA

(Meaning) Morningstar.

DA • NI • QUE

(Meaning) God is my judge.

How can I
blaze and blind
like a brightening
morningstar
when there is a God
that judges my
every sparkle

> - *even my name carries conflict*

CONTENTS

CHAPTER I
THE COLLAPSING.......1

CHAPTER II
THE EXPLODING……..63

CHAPTER III
THE BURNING………...127

EPILOGUE……………..199

CHAPTER I
THE COLLAPSING

Hurricane

She was a
day spun of soft silk
and a hurricane soul.

Away From Home

I will return

with a head
full of memories

with a body
full of love

and a heart
full of secrets.

Hiraeth

Be quiet my soul
stop making me long
for a home I
have never known.

And we fill the air with I love you's
until it loses all its meaning and replaces
that what we are so afraid to say

- *it is over*

Don't Want To Let Go

No one ever tells you
about the breakups

where no one is fighting
and where you just want
to keep on holding.

Under Water

What was it like to let him go?

Letting him go was like taking
a breath of fresh air, only to realize
I was still under water.

People

Religion taught me
that the biggest crime
was falling in love
with people rather
than gender.

Chronical Restlessness

Is it my curse that I will

always
want
more?

Love Letters (pt. 1)

My love, I would hold on
to you forever but we were
carved from a different star

and as we fell to this earth
the trail of our dust might
have touched but you and I
we speak a different language

I will never truly know you
and you will never truly
know me

because we were made
of a different home.

Water & Stardust

You were like
the running water of
a creek

steady and calm
your way carved out and ever
the same

and I was like the sparkle
of the sun dancing on your
current like the reflection of a
million stars

restless and unpredictable
but how magnificent
we looked

but sunrays come and go
warming many places and
many hearts

and while you were waiting
for the dawn to return
I realized that water and
stardust never truly can
become one.

Disappear

I make no excuse
for the way I decide
to disappear out
of people's lives

like I have never
been there at all.

Monster In My Bed

I wonder when I turned
into that monster I read about

in the poems
of the hurt and the heartbroken.

Crossroad

I feel like I'm on a crossroad
to my left there is a life of comfort
of safety and stability
to my right there is a life of passion
of fire and uncertainty.

I feel like I'm on a crossroad
and each path will take its toll
one has the power to burn me alive
the other to slowly kill my soul.

Soulmates

Soulmates
aren't the ones
that stay forever

soulmates
are the ones
that cause
a thunder
in your soul
a chaos
in your bones

then disappear to
reveal the damage
of the storm

and leave you
yearning for more.

Leaving You Blind

I will lighten
up your night sky
like a blazing morningstar

and the moment you
realize I'm not a dream
I will be gone.

Being addicted to experiences
is the most dangerous addiction of all
because I'm addicted to everything

- *always afraid of missing out*

Storm

Consider me the storm
of your dreams.

Guilt

My entire life I was taught that
my virginity was something special
for years as I opened my legs
instead of honey guilt poured out

when I tried to tell you this
you made it seem like a good thing
because maybe next time it would
stop me from sharing something
that was only meant for a man
and a woman within the walls
of a marriage

but that marriage never came
because I never could.

Destruction

I caused destruction
to every soul that
ever loved me

I burn their temples down
before they get to mine
because I know I don't have
half-sided love to give.

Once they convert me
I will throw myself on
their altar of self-sacrifice

so I become their downfall
before I become my own
because destroying myself
that I fear most of all.

My body realized this was ending
long before my mind did

- *I no longer want you to touch me*

Monstrosity

How have I
ever been capable
of this monstrosity
called hurting you.

Your Pain

I imagine your pain
by imagining *him*
leaving me the way

I left you.

Is this longing and wandering
what is truly means to be human

- *what if nothing will ever satisfy me*

Fall

We make love
like we are about
to fall

you holding on tight
and I turned away

not able to look at
you before I let go.

Lilies

Remember the lilies
you bought me that
stained your jacket

just like the lily stains
the memory of you
won't fade away

and just like
your jacket we
were beyond saving.

Milky Way

And suddenly you have
taken an entire galaxy
and left me with an
empty space in my bed

leaving me begging
you to stay as I reach
for a darkness of nothing
where there once was
a whole Milky Way.

Promises

After you I promised myself
to be careful with my promises
but even that promise I could
not keep.

Red Pants

I saw pants in the color
you love today

they were waving
from a white picket fence
the kind we never got to have

it was like seeing a ghost of you
reminding me of my crimes
and how I destroyed you

until you were nothing but dust
leaving nothing but an empty pair
of jeans.

Summer Day

I met you as a summer day
you left me as a hurricane.

The Collapsing

This is the memory of us.
You keep asking me why I chose you
but the reality is, I didn't.

I don't know how it's possible that
even when we love a person so much
we are still capable of hurting them.

Just like I don't know why autumn smells
like new beginnings and the sound of October
was actually the sound of me leaving you.

The wind carries your question over
continents.
Why.
How can I ever explain this feeling to you, my
love?
It's a hideous thing realizing you are living a
life that no longer belongs to you.

How can I tell someone as innocent as an
April breeze that their love is suffocating me.
How can I tell you I do not want the house,
the marriage, the Sunday church sessions, the
mind numbing conversations that carry no
challenge.

I've heard all the warnings and now I've
ignored them and suddenly it's four years later
and tomorrow is today and I'm
in the midst of this life I've never wanted.

Everyone always believes they are doing the
right thing, until they are not.
The truth is, there is no religion or story that
can save me now.
Not even the one of you and me.

You see, I wasn't your
happily ever after.

Darling, I was your catalyst.

CHAPTER II
THE EXPLODING

Stunningly Dangerous

She was stunningly dangerous
and just out of reach.

Starlight

There was one
who fell in love with the starlight
in my eyes but then decided that
loving a universe just wasn't for him.

You entered me
looked around
then wiped your
feet on the doormat
of my being

and left this place
a little emptier
than it was before

- *you never made a home out of me*

Kindness

When he tells me he can't
see me be anything but kind
I smile at him and wonder
if he would be afraid of
the hurricane inside my soul
and the fire inside my bones.

Wolf-skinned Girl

Beware
of the wolf-skinned girls
they will make no apologies
on how they decide
to devour you.

How can I tell men
the baring of her skin
is not an invitation
or consent

when her same
nakedness
threatens me as if
it takes away from
my own beauty

> - *there is room for growth with women too*

Two Lovers

Have you ever fallen
for two people
have you ever had
your heart divided in two

have you ever possessed
two lovers in which one
is reason and the other

simply every other part
of you.

Rivers of stardust
are flowing
through my veins

my mind is made
of galaxies you
have yet to discover

my skin burns
with the fire
of a thousand suns

I'm not here
for your comfort

I was never made
to make life
easier for you

I was created to make you
doubt the core of your
very existence -

to make you question how
any other love ever satisfied
you before

> - *don't try to turn me into something
>   comfortable*

Love Letters (pt. 2)

My love, would you still want me
if you would see the damage to my soul
if you would see me wide awake at night
trying to get my demons under control.

If you would know that behind that smile
lighting up a room
there is an awful lot of darkness of a girl
that had to grow up too soon.

Hell

And he showed me that hell
could be a such a pretty place.

Holy

What made men so holy
that two women loving each other
is either a sin or a dirty fantasy.

Ex-lovers

You're skipping through
radio stations like they are
your ex-lovers.

Modern Love

I look at every picture
and I scroll through every feed
needing proof of your existence

I reread all our messages
and look for clues to where you are

(who you are with)

in momentary photos that disappear
within seconds

(together with my heart)

blue checks and no response
turn my stomach into knots
in the silence I fear you stopped
thinking of me.

Sirens

She was the kind of girl
that listened to the sirens
and let herself be lured in

by the promise of something
beautiful.

Bored

You talk about politics, but I have long since lost my interest. Sleep is paralyzing me together with my half satisfied body and too much alcohol for my blood.
You have to call me a cab, you tell me. I catch myself wishing that cab would drive you out of my existence completely.

You left fingerprints on my skin, but I have long since lost my interest. There is no trace of the person that spoke of writing and art now your desires are fulfilled. I catch myself wondering why I gave myself to you. I try not to regret and to remember the pleasure disguised as happiness.

You make another joke I don't understand, but I have long since lost my interest. Another comment about Trump that makes you unpopular among your friends. How you love to hear yourself talk to no end. You never really saw me, just my body. And frankly, I'm bored.

How come whole cultures and religions
are built to make sure I keep my legs closed

- *what are they afraid of*

Sad Girls

You will regret me in the morning
because without the wine-stained
kisses sad girls like me suddenly
taste awfully bitter.

Freedom & Fear

He would never
truly capture the
essence of her wildness

because she tasted
of freedom where he
tasted of fear

and even the stars
couldn't keep up
with her.

Just because I opened my legs for you
doesn't mean I have opened the gate
to all that is me

- *I am more than my vagina*

The Sea And Her Stars

You can't kiss promises into my lips
and be surprised when I turn them
to words

you don't taunt the sea
when you know you can't handle
her waves

you don't beg for the stars
when you know you can't bear
their light.

Love Letters (pt. 3)

My love,
what a dangerous thing
to love a poet
but how magnificent
to be loved by one.

Young God

He will have me worship him
on the altar of his words

he will have me pray to the
empty loneliness of old lovers
begging them to release me
from this heaven turned hell

and just when I think he
might be no God after all
he has me back on my knees

taking in my old religion
like it is my new.

Thief

You can keep my heart
but please give me back
my sleep.

A Taste Of Stardust

I told you to be careful
where you take those lips
because they all want to know
what stardust tastes like
on their tongue

until they realize it's not easy
to keep up with something that
was created in the heavens

with something that was created
to be wild.

Questions

Why is it you feel this
uncontrollable need
to correct my wrongs
when I'm learning

to change my visions
when they don't align
with yours

to shield me from all
the mistakes you once
made too

would it truly be
so terrible if I
turned out to be

just
like
you.

A Universal Warning

Make no mistake my darling
a kiss of the sun can be gentle
like a lover's touch
but treat her carelessly
and she will burn you

only when the moon stops
shining she will be missed
and only when you wake up
in a starless sky you will hear
the darkness whisper
I told you so

make no mistake, my darling
for one day you might find yourself

burnt
surrounded by darkness
and alone.

Apologies

I refuse to be one of those girls
saying sorry for speaking her mind
the kind of soft spoken apologies
because she might be

too much
too soon
all at once.

Bravery

I think of my mother who
stopped her engagement to
that other man so she could be free

I think of my father who pulled
himself out of that other life so he
could be who he was meant to be

and realize their bravery is the
root of what created me.

Plot Twist

You kept repeating
it's like a movie
and that was all
I was to you

a plot twist

to keep
your life
interesting.

Jealousy

He made cigarette smoke
look like elusive flowers
and I was jealous of the wind
that got to carry his breath away.

The Exploding

This is about you and me and the story
that never existed.
My entire life I've been taught that
things are black and white.

That there's a right and wrong.
A heaven and hell.

But nothing and no one is just one thing.
It goes against every rule of the universe.
It's an insult to all its beauty and
complications.
You were my hell and my heaven.

Even among all the doubt and the guilt
you made my life infinitely better.

I wanted a change, but you can't light a fire
without burning something.
A star can't be born before exploding first.
I couldn't get to him before going through
you.

You taught me it's alright to share with
somebody and not be in love with them.
You were a dream in the making, a ghost
for the taking. Thinking back of you now
you don't seem real and that is ok.

Through you I taught myself to be brave
and that it's alright to make mistakes.
That sometimes you don't need promises
and forevers to make a meaningful
connection.

It was simply your world versus mine
and you and me always somewhere in
between.

Until we were nothing.
Until we were *everything*.

CHAPTER III
THE BURNING

Danica Gim

Midsummer Dangerous

And there he was –

night sky beauty and
midsummer danger.

My Dark Prince

His eyes hold a thousand and one sandstorms
his sun-kissed skin a thousand and one stories
his raven hair a thousand and one night skies

and all I can think is that touching him must
feel like holding a thousand and one universes.

Girl Of Shadows

He called me a girl
of shadows
but kissed me
anyway.

Riot

If you decide to love me
let it be for the riots in me.

Mine

It's a strange moment
when your heart returns
to you

like he never took it
in the first place

it always belonged
to myself first of all.

Touched

I need to be touched
every hour
every second
of every day

if not by your hands
by your mind

if not by your lips
by your soul.

I want something that borders on insanity
I want to feel your fingers inside of me
I want to fight with you repeatedly
to feel your soul so passionately

    - I was not made for something ordinary

Dangerous Sweetness

It's your eyes- he told me.
They are made of honey, created with the sole purpose to lure me in.

Bookstore

I watched him walk through a thousand stories. I followed how his fingertips briefly touched the backs of other worlds.

I stared as he moved from tragedy to history, from history to poetry.

And suddenly I understood every love story ever written, understood each poem's sweet agony.

In that moment I realized what it was like to have two souls collide with such an impact that you can still taste their stardust from a distance.

Kiss of Death

He kisses promises into my mouth
and fears into my heart I didn't even
know existed.

Sacrifice

Let's sacrifice our
love on the altar
of star-crossed lovers
because nothing fucks
as perfect as holy ground.

Imagine

I imagine endless futures with you
sceneries of lush green hills
in countries that might not even exist.

I imagine wine-stained lips kissing my pale
breasts whispering about lovers that found
death because they were never as lucky as us.

I envision our skins pressed together
yours made of copper, mine made of milk.
I think of the wrinkles that will cover them
one day.

I envision caressing those lines that betray
the travels of places we have yet to see
while you tell me you would do it all over
again.

Oceans & Mountains

His skin holds the ink
of oceans and mountains
of travels to me
so unknown.

I know his hands
have loved someone
before he made
of me a home

his touch sends
to my fingertips
an explosion
of a thousand stars

and I know
I will have to learn
what it's like
to love him from afar.

Goodbye

I don't know why each goodbye keeps getting harder, I cried.

Because each time your feelings have grown stronger, he replied.

Out Of Time

Every time I meet your gaze
I wonder what I will find

that starlight in your eyes that says
I can't believe she is mine

or that night sky full of sadness
when you realize we are running
out of time.

No Pretty Words

When I saw you
for the first time
my mind wasn't
filled with pretty
words

my lips didn't
overflow
with poetry
or prose

rather one
simple thought

fuck -
here I go.

Constellations

He traced my birthmarks
and found constellations.

The Things He Says To Me (pt. 1)

You are unattainable. Once you are gone I only remember how you feel, not what you look like.

My soul is in love with the memory of yours and only when you are right in front of me I perceive you as someone that is real.

I try to memorize every mark, every curve and every scar. Every single angle that makes you who you are.
But once you leave you are as elusive as the wind, your image escapes me like water running through my fingers.

Until I see you again, I'm either loving the ghost of you or the you I once perceived when we were both still made of the stars alone.

Forgotten Promises

Oh and what a delicious boy he is
tasting of sunrays and forgotten promises.

Thinking Of You

I draw the traces
of forgotten oceans
the waves mimicking
the softness of my breasts

imitating the curves of
the unexplored landscapes
of my body and I think of you

                I think of you

                              thinking of you.

First Time

When he told me
he loved me
for the first time
he repeated it
like a prayer

like a newfound religion
an undiscovered fear
an unfulfilled wish.

Immortality

He told her he wanted
to be remembered
she told him she was
afraid to be forgotten.

He sat there with his camera
and she with her pen
and through film and paper
they made each other immortal.

With Kisses

He laid me down between
the poems and whispered:

I'm going to make love to you with kisses.

The Things He Says To Me (pt. 2)

He told me that the sun had turned
my porcelain skin into a golden milk
and how he could not wait to drink from it.

Serenity

And in the middle of
all its unease and unrest
missing you has a strange
kind of serenity to it

simply because
I know you exist.

Nostalgia

I'm tasting the sunrays
of a distant childhood memory
one that was happy

there is a familiarity in his voice
like I heard it before in another life
and my entire soul is wide awake
when he talks.

Enough

I have so much love to give
I've always wondered
if I was made to love
just one person

until I met you
suddenly even
all my love
didn't seem enough.

Sunday Morning

You told me I felt like a Sunday morning
warming your bones with a watery golden sun
and the sound of chirping birds
invisible but ever present

you told me I felt like a Sunday morning
with the looming threat of a tomorrow that
seems to never come

a dream like state in which you forget your
own name but that reminds you of a
childhood memory of t-shirts covered in ice
cream stains.

Familiarity

When you read to me
I realize your voice
is the only one my soul
has ever truly known.

Religion

I'm the only religion
I'm interested in

If I'm going to
exclude people
let it be to heal
myself

if I'm to love
with limits
let it be to learn
to love
without

if I'm supposed
to be confined
by rules written
by men
let it be to start
a riot that can
burn it all
down.

Moon-skinned Girl

I knew they were wrong
comparing me to oceans
and storms

when I realized I first
loved a man who loved
me too much and now
love a man that doesn't
love me enough

I'm like the moon
nothing without the sun
fading in and out of her
lover's touch

always changing her
mind not knowing
what is good for herself.

We Will Meet Again

We never cried on our way to the airport
instead we laughed like never before

as if the ominous cloud of our nearing
goodbye made us fearless instead of paralyzed.

We didn't shed a single tear as we kissed
farewell under the dawning morning sun.

and the unspoken words echoed through
our touch as I turned my back to you

we will meet again
we will meet again

we will meet again.

Reminder

And I will remind
myself I carved a
way through the
stars to get to you.

The Burning

This is me imagining you.
All messy raven haired, making me tea
and telling me to eat better.
For a long time I felt nothing and now
I'm burning and I realize I'm one of
the lucky ones.

I don't take love for granted anymore.
No longer I assume that things last forever
and I've accepted that it is no crime
to change.

People shed their skins like snakes
and it takes a while for them to grow
comfortable with their new ones,
but more than anything it takes others
a while to accept you are no longer
the person they made you out to be.

Lately I open my eyes and think I'm back
in California with you. The sun burning my
skin and the heat making me dizzy while
I stare at you like *you* are saving me instead
of *me* saving myself.

I think of Vancouver in the frost when
your face was still unknown to me
and I still thought I was going back

home unchanged.

I'm getting used to this fire in my lungs
and every day I pray it can burn a little
longer, a little brighter.

Anything to keep this feeling from
going away. Anything to keep me
from going back to the prison I created
for myself. The one where I felt nothing.
The one where I was numb.

Sometimes I look at you and I don't
know who you are. I expect you to
disappear like you are some illusion
my mind conjured up to make my life
bearable again.

But you always stay, against all of
my expectations. I think it's because
this is the first time in my life I feel
like I have no control.

Every day you feel a little bit
different from the person I first met.
Just like I feel a little different every day,
from the person I thought myself to be.

Yet you are the same. I catch myself

wondering who's life I'm living.
No person can be this happy.

I guess this is simply you and me,
finding each other against all odds.

Epilogue

It is going to be a hard year. The kind that
changes you for good.

If we hadn't been so afraid of hurting people
we would have hurt so much less of them.

Don't believe the stories. Told by others
or by yourself. Making mistakes doesn't
make you evil. Yes, they will crucify you,
label you. It is human nature, love.
Making an example out of your wrongs
is how they feel better about their own.

But in the end, each of us is human.
All excruciatingly imperfect.
Was this where you were so afraid of?

The sun is still burning.
The moon is still returning.
The stars still kiss you goodnight.
Except now you are free.
Of him, but mostly of yourself.

That is what we learned, isn't it?
We don't need to collapse,
to explode or burn to the ground
to finally find the courage to make
a significant change.

We always had the strength to do so.

So remember when it happens again,
it isn't a crime to fail. Just be honest
next time. You aren't the kind of girl
to live quietly. You have been compared
to many things and storms and hurricanes
are always one of them. You shed your skin
best in a collision of chaos. That is how *you*
grow.

You either love wild, or not at all.

ABOUT THE AUTHOR

Danique Gimbrère is a Dutch writer, born in the Netherlands, where her first novel was published at the age of seventeen. Danique temporarily moved to Vancouver at twenty-three, where she created an anonymous Instagram account under the name 'Danica Gim' and started sharing her poetry. In less than a year the account gained tens of thousands of followers worldwide, making Danica Gim her better known pen name. Her work has been praised for her raw and relatable lines as she writes about various topics many young people encounter in life.

Printed in France by Amazon
Brétigny-sur-Orge, FR